Published by Top That! Publishing plc
Tide Mill Way, Woodbridge, Suffolk, IP12 1AP, UK
www.topthatpublishing.com
Copyright © 2013 Top That! Publishing plc
All rights reserved
0 2 4 6 8 9 7 5 3 1
Printed and bound in China

Creative Director – Simon Couchman
Editorial Director – Daniel Graham

Written by Kate Thomson
Illustrated by Daniel Howarth

ISBN 978-1-78244-357-5

A catalogue record for this book is available from the British Library
Printed and bound in China

The Giant Quest

Written by Kate Thomson

Illustrated by Daniel Howarth

One morning the kingdom awoke with a fright,
A giant had been making noise all through the night.
He could still be heard sobbing and thumping his chest,
The villagers needed a knight to go on a quest.

A knight called Geoffrey stepped up and declared,
'I'll stop this giant, I'm not scared!'
Dressed in armour, with a sword and a shield,
He followed the noise and marched over a field.

Over rocks and boulders, past hedges and weeds,
Geoffrey hiked forward with his noble steed.
The giant continued to roar and wail,
As Geoffrey trekked further along the trail.

The brave knight walked past bushes, shrubs and trees,
The giant howled and gulped, then sniffed and sneezed!
Up and down hills Geoffrey ventured far and wide,
Getting closer and closer to the giant that cried.

Suddenly, Geoffrey realised something was wrong,
There was no noise at all, not even birdsong!
The noisy giant? Where could he be?
Geoffrey looked everywhere, then what did he see?

A huge, hairy giant is what Geoffrey saw!
With large ears and a great big beard on his jaw!
But then a teardrop fell down the giant's cheek,
So brave Geoffrey decided to stay and speak.

'Why are you sad?' he asked the giant up high,
Whilst dodging the teardrops that fell from the sky.
'I'm lonely and lost,' the giant said, with a roar.
'My family's gone; they're not here anymore.'

'Let's find them,' said the daring knight.
'We'll search the kingdom; it'll be all right!'

Past trees and rocks and
enormous boulders,
Geoffrey perched up high
on the giant's shoulders.
Whilst holding on tight to
the giant's hair,
An unlikely friendship
grew between the pair.

The new friends looked out
across the land,
Smiling, the giant shook
Geoffrey's hand.
'Thank you Geoffrey, you've
found my family!'
Take a look at the picture –
how many giants can you see?

Can you help to spot the giant's family?